WHERE'S OUR MAMA?

Où Est Maman?

DIANE GOODE

RED FOX

for my mama

with grateful acknowledgment
to Lucia Monfried

A Red Fox Book

Published by Random House Children's Books
20 Vauxhall Bridge Road, London SW1V 2SA

A division of Random House UK Ltd
London Melbourne Sydney Auckland
Johannesburg and agencies throughout the world

First published in the United States 1991 by Dutton Children's Books Inc. New York as Where's Mama?

First published in Great Britain by Andersen Press 1992

Red Fox edition 1993

Printed in Hong Kong

RANDOM HOUSE UK Limited Reg. No. 954009

ISBN 0 09 999170 5

When we arrived in the station, a big gust of wind blew Mama's hat right off her head. "Oh, la la!" she cried. "Stay right here while I find it."

A notre arrivée à la gare, un violent coup de vent emporte le chapeau de Maman. "Oh, la la! Ne bougez pas, les enfants, je vais le chercher."

Mama ran after her hat
while we sat and waited,
and waited.

Pendant que Maman
court derrière son chapeau,
nous nous asseyons . . . et nous attendons.

When Mama still did not return, we began to cry.
A gendarme nearby heard us.
"We have lost our mother," we sobbed.
"What is her name?" he asked.
"Mama."
"What does your mama look like?"
"Our mama is the most beautiful woman in the world!"
"Dry your eyes, children, and we will find her."

Comme Maman ne revient pas,
nous commençons à pleurer.
Un gendarme qui passe par là,
nous entend sangloter.
"Nous avons perdu notre maman."
"Comment s'appelle-t-elle?"
"Maman."
"Comment est-elle?"
"Notre maman est la plus belle femme du monde!"
"Séchez vos larmes, les enfants,
nous allons la retrouver."

"Is this your mama?" asked the gendarme.
"Oh, no, sir. Our mama is very strong.
Mama can carry her own parcels."

"Est-ce votre maman?"
"Oh, non, Monsieur. Notre maman est très forte.
Elle porte ses paquets elle-même."

"Is this your mama?"
"Oh, no, sir. Our mama doesn't read the newspaper. Mama reads books—millions of books."

"Est-ce votre maman?"
"Oh, non, Monsieur. Notre maman ne lit pas le journal. Elle lit des livres, des millions de livres."

FOLIES
PARIS
PHOTO
UHU
JOURNAL
LA LINGERIE
VOGU
FEMME
MONTE
SPORTS
VUE

SILENCE!
SAVEZ-VOUS?

"Is this your mama?"
"Oh, no, sir. Our mama never whispers.
Everyone loves Mama's voice—she is
famous for it."

"Est-ce votre maman?"
"Oh, non, Monsieur.
Notre maman ne parle jamais tout bas.
Elle parle haut et fort. Tout le monde admire sa voix."

"Is that your mama?"
"Oh, no, sir. Our mama is very slim. But
Mama cooks the best food in the world."

"Est-ce votre maman?"
"Oh, non, Monsieur. Notre maman est très mince,
pourtant elle cuisine les meilleurs plats du monde."

AGA

"Is this your mama?"
"Oh, no, sir. Our mama wears only pretty hats."

"Est-ce votre maman?"
"Oh, non, Monsieur.
Notre maman ne porte que des beaux chapeaux."

"Is that your mama?"
"Oh, no, sir. Our mama is not afraid of a mouse. Mama is very brave."

"Est-ce votre maman?"
"Oh, non, Monsieur.
Notre maman n'a pas peur d'une souris.

"Is that your mama?"
"Oh, no, sir. Our mama would never do that. She is very clever."

"Est-ce votre maman?"
"Oh, non, Monsieur.
Notre maman ne ferait jamais cela.
Elle est très raisonnable."

"Is that your mama?"
"Oh, no, sir. People listen when our mama speaks. Oh! I just remembered what Mama said."

"Est-ce votre maman?"
"Oh, non, Monsieur. Quand notre maman parle, tout le monde l'écoute.
Oh! Je me souviens . . ."

OCTOBRE
NOVEMBRE
1
2
3

24

"Mama said we were to wait at the station."

"Maman avait dit
que nous devions l'attendre à la gare!"

PARIS AUSTERLITZ
EXPRESS

SUD-EXPRESS
BORDEAUX-MADRID

“Is this your mama?”

"Est-ce votre maman?"

"Yes, this is our mama!"

"Maman!"